THE REVOLTING
BABY

THE REVOLTING
BABY

MARY HOOPER

ILLUSTRATIONS BY
FREDERIQUE VAYSSIERE

BLOOMSBURY

Published in Great Britain in 2008 by Bloomsbury Publishing Plc
36 Soho Square, London, W1D 3QY

First published in the UK by Blackie Children's Books, 1993

A CIP catalogue record of this book is available from the
British Library

ISBN 978 0 7475 8613 5

All papers used by Bloomsbury Publishing are natural, recyclable products made
from wood grown in well-managed forests. The manufacturing processes conform to
the environmental regulations of the country of origin.

Typeset by Dorchester Typesetting Group Ltd
Printed in Great Britain by Clays Ltd, St Ives Plc

1 3 5 7 9 10 8 6 4 2

www.maryhooper.co.uk
www.bloomsbury.com/childrens

chapter one

'And who's the sweetest little coochie-woochie?' I heard Mum cooing from her bedroom, and then came loud, smacky kissing noises.

I sat bolt upright in bed, wondering what was going on. I didn't think I'd heard Dad called a coochie-woochie before – and besides, he was in

France on business.

'And isn't it the cutest little woffle dumpling in the world?' Mum cooed on, and, knowing that Dad had definitely never been called a woffle dumpling, I remembered: we were looking after Emily, who was my sister Helen's baby. She and her husband Christopher had gone away to a posh hotel on the coast somewhere to celebrate their second wedding anniversary.

I rolled out of bed and went into Mum's room, wrapped in my duvet. Mum had got Emily out of the portable cot Helen and Christopher had brought with them, and was bouncing her up and down on the bed.

'And who's got the biggest blue eyes and the . . . Katie, please don't trail that duvet along the floor in the dirt,' she said, not looking up.

'I didn't think the floor was dirty,' I said. 'You're always telling me you've just cleaned it.'

'That's as may be,' Mum said. She sat Emily down on the bed in front of her. 'Oh, do look. She's terribly ticklish. You've only got to lift your finger and nearly tickle her tummy and she starts chortling with laughter.'

'Fancy,' I said, glancing towards the roly-poly
bundle of baby clothes that was Emily. She was
quite sweet, but if Mum was going to be soppy all
day it was going to get on my nerves. 'I'm starv-
ing. Can we have sausages for breakfast?'

'First Emily has to have a bath and her breakfast,' Mum said. She started speaking in a silly
high voice again. 'And Emily doesn't like
sausages, do you, my poppety bundle? Emily likes
scrambled egg, very runny, and warm milk.'

I was practically sick on the spot. 'I think I'll go
and get dressed,' I said, making for the door.

'Come over and hold her, Katie!'

Grudgingly, unwillingly, I went over.

'And here's poppety bundle's Auntie Katie!' Mum said, picking her up and dropping her into my arms. 'Smile at her!' Mum directed. 'Give her a little coochie-coo under the chin and she'll gurgle back at you.'

I rolled my eyes. 'Please!' I said, but nevertheless, just to humour Mum, I tickled Emily under the chin and she broke into a two-toothed grin. 'Yes. Very nice,' I said. 'What else can she do?'

'Oh, hundreds of things,' Mum said. 'She can wave bye-bye and say "Da-da" and shuffle along the floor on her bottom and play pat-a-cake.'

'Very useful,' I said. 'How is she on cooking sausages?'

Mum tutted. 'Don't be silly, Katie. I thought you'd take an interest in her. You are her auntie, after all.'

I shrugged nonchalantly. 'She's all right,' I said. 'I just happen to think one person at a time going batty over her is enough.'

But Mum had gone off again. 'And have you seen the little tiddy bear blow raspberries?' she gushed, blowing out her own cheeks something alarming.

'Well, no, not lately . . .' I said, rolling my eyes to myself.

Mum paused from the raspberries, took Emily back and sniffed her. 'And after raspberries, how about botties? Shall we give doodle-kins a nice clean bottie?' Mum looked up at me briefly. 'Pass that basket with the nappies in, please, Katie. And then could you stand by to take the dirty –'

Well, I was out of that bedroom in double quick

time, I can tell you. I shoved the basket at Mum and ran back to my room.

It was Saturday and there was quite a lot going on. Flicka, who'd been a bridesmaid with me at Helen and Christopher's wedding, was coming to see Emily, and Mrs Bailey, Emily's other granny – I always called her Mrs Bayleaf – was also coming to see Emily to make sure she was being brought up properly (I'd heard Mum call her an interfering old bat). As well as this Mum and I had to take Emily to the photographer's studio in town in the afternoon; Mum was having a proper studio portrait of the baby taken as a surprise for Helen.

I was downstairs looking at the sausages and wondering what they tasted like raw, when the phone in the hall rang. It was Helen, wanting a minute-by-minute account of what Emily had done the previous evening. I shouted to Mum to pick up the upstairs extension and then, a bit later, just as Mum came into the kitchen with Emily in a clean pink-and-white something called an angel top and white towelling tights, it rang again. Emily gave a yell in competition with it.

'Get the phone, will you, Katie?' Mum said,

strapping Emily into her high chair with one hand and getting an egg out of the fridge with the other. 'Does little possums want her breakfast then?'

It was Gran – a very faint and peculiar-sounding Gran. 'Is your mother there?' she whispered, whereas she normally wants to know what I'm doing at school and if we've seen Emily and hundreds of other things before she asks for Mum.

I passed her over. Mum pointed me in the direction of a mixing bowl and told me to beat up an egg, then went into the hall and shut the door so that she could hear Gran over Emily's hungry yells.

I'd beaten the egg so well that the work surface was freckled orange when Mum came back into the kitchen, without her coochie-coo face on, and said Gran had had an accident.

'She's tripped over something in the garden and thinks she's broken her leg,' she said worriedly. 'A neighbour's with her and the ambulance is coming, but she wants me at the hospital. They're bound to keep her in . . .'

I stared at Mum. 'But what about Emily?' I

said. 'What about us?'

Mum stood in the doorway, biting her lip. 'Well, obviously I can't take you both with me.' She suddenly dived for the notebook next to the phone. 'I'll just have to get Helen and Christopher back.'

'But they're having lunch somewhere posh, aren't they? And going to a stately home this afternoon and having dinner tonight . . .'

'Can't be helped,' Mum said briskly, going out and picking up the phone. 'If they start off now, they can be back in an hour and a half.'

I gave Emily a chunk of bread and she started gnawing on it. 'But what about –'

'I've got to go to Gran,' Mum said firmly. 'She'll be terrified on her own – she hates hospitals. It's a shame about their anniversary treat but they've already had half of it and I know Helen would want me to be with Gran.'

She dialled the number of the hotel. 'I hope they haven't booked out already . . .' she muttered. 'Helen and Christopher Bailey, please,' she said briskly into the receiver. 'Yes, it's quite urgent.'

There was a long pause and then Mum said, 'Oh

dear! Well, can you get them to ring home straightaway, please. The minute they appear.'

She put the phone down. 'They've had breakfast and they've gone for a walk in the grounds,' she said, putting butter into a saucepan and pouring what was left of the egg on top. 'Get my bag, will you, love? . . . Find the car keys . . . Cut a slice of bread into fingers . . . Hand me my jacket,' she went on, stirring the mixture in the saucepan while Emily dropped soggy bits of bread all round her high chair. 'There's a train on the hour . . . D'you think you can manage without me until they get home?'

'Of course I can,' I said. I looked at Emily, now pushing bread pellets into her ears. 'It's only a baby, isn't it? I can look after a baby. They can't *do* anything . . .'

'She's only making grizzly noises because she's hungry . . . I'll take the car and leave it outside the station . . . You spoon-feed her with this . . .' She shoved the saucepan at me.

I sat down in front of Emily. 'Not straight out of the saucepan, Katie!' Mum screeched. 'Now, when Helen rings tell her what's happened and

ask them to drive home straightaway.'

'Right!'

She flew back from the door. 'I forgot to say goodbye to my baby!' she said, tickling Emily under the chin.

'Please!' I said. 'You're distracting her from her food.'

'Are you sure you can manage?'

'Of course.'

'If you're in trouble, ask Laura next door. Her Jamie's the same age as Emily.'

'I won't need to do that,' I said with dignity.

'And if you —'

'You'll miss your train, Mum,' I said. 'Just go!'

So she went.

chapter two

'There's a lovely . . . er . . . coochie baby,' I said, looking round to make sure the cat couldn't hear me.

Emily's mouth widened for a yell and, as Mum drove off down the road, I quickly popped a spoonful of revolting runny scrambled egg in.

'There, isn't that lovely?' I said, my tummy heaving at the sight of it. I picked a piece of eggshell off the next spoonful. 'And here's another lovely mouthful for the . . . er . . . woochie bunny wunny.'

Emily swallowed the egg and made a lipsmacking sound. I unstuck a piece of bread from between her fingers and waved it tantalisingly in front of her. 'And what about a bread and butter finger?' I looked at it again. 'Well, bread and butter splodge.'

Emily chomped it down with her two teeth, smiled a gummy smile and then opened her mouth wide for another mouthful. I popped it in, she chomped . . . and the whole process was repeated over and over again until the egg and bread were done for.

Well, I thought, taking the bowl to the sink and looking at Emily with satisfaction, that was easy. Whoever said that looking after babies was hard work? Helen made such a fuss about being totally exhausted all the time and being desperate for a break, but now I could actually see what having a baby was like. And it was a doddle. I bet

I could look after it without getting exhausted. I bet I could look after five, no trouble. I could probably run a playgroup, single-handed.

Emily cooed to herself, dried egg along her top lip and bread in her ears – a ready-made snack for later, I thought. I lifted her out of the high chair and she wiped sticky hands on me, but it didn't matter, because I was only wearing my third-best tracksuit. I sat her on the floor, remembering to put cushions round her in case she toppled over, and the phone rang.

'Just ringing from the station,' Mum said. 'Is everything all right?'

'Of course it's all right!' I said. 'You only left thirty seconds ago.'

'What's Emily doing?'

I sighed. 'She's eaten all her egg and bread and now we're just going to sit quietly and play.'

'Has Helen rung yet?'

'Not yet,' I said. 'And don't sound so fussed, Mum. I can manage perfectly well until she gets here.'

'You will keep Emily clean, won't you?' Mum said. 'I don't want her to look messy when Helen arrives. And don't tell Mrs Bailey you were managing on your own – and you'd better ring the photographer and cancel our sitting.'

'All right, all right, got to go . . .' I said, because Emily had started shuffling along the floor towards the cat.

'Why have you got to go? What's happening?'

'Nothing at all!' I said. 'Give my love to Gran. Bye!'

I put the phone down and rescued the cat – but not before Emily had grabbed a handful of its fur.

'Mustn't touch!' I said, picking fur from between Emily's sticky fingers. 'And how did you get butter in your hair?'

I picked more butter, fur and a dollop of egg from the angel top. It wasn't looking quite so angelic as it had done, so I went to the bathroom for a wet flannel. It was new, though, and green, and left a pale green streak behind it all down the white lacy front of the angel top. But then if she wasn't having her photograph taken it didn't really matter.

Shame, really, I thought. Mum had been looking forward to surprising Helen with a big framed photograph. And it was a shame that Helen and Christopher had to miss the final bit of their anniversary treat, too . . .

Just as I thought that the phone rang.

'It's me!' Helen said breathlessly. 'The hotel said to ring urgently. What on earth's wrong? Is it Emily? What's the matter?'

I opened my mouth to tell her what the matter was – but something happened to the words while they were on their way out. You see, what I suddenly thought was: why couldn't I manage on my own for the day? Why couldn't I take Emily to the photographer's? This thought hit me and then I said, 'Nothing's wrong. Nothing's the matter.'

Helen tutted. 'Then why on earth did Mum — put her on, will you, Katie?' she said impatiently, meaning that she wasn't going to bother to speak to me any longer. It was that impatient voice of hers which really decided me. I could manage perfectly well on my own, I'd show them!

'Mum's busy,' I said with dignity. 'Mum's busy . . . er . . . talking.' Well, wherever she was, she was bound to be talking. I fixed an eagle eye on Emily; she was shuffling towards a log basket which was supposed to live in the sitting room but hadn't quite got there. I stretched the phone line to its utmost length but, although I could see most of the kitchen, I couldn't reach her.

'What d'you mean?' Helen demanded. 'Talking to Laura-next-door, d'you mean? What did she ring for, then?'

I crossed my fingers. 'Um . . . because she didn't know whether to put salt on Emily's scrambled egg.'

'What?!'

I waved to try and attract Emily's attention. She'd put her fingers through a hole in the basket, though, and wasn't looking. Still, she couldn't do much harm to a log basket, could she? 'She . . . er . . . wasn't sure if babies liked it or not,' I said in a distracted voice.

'But the hotel said it was *urgent*!'

'It was urgent,' I said. 'Mum wanted to get it right.'

'For goodness' sake!' Helen said, and sighed. 'Well, anyway, she doesn't have salt.'

'That's just what I told Mum!' I stifled a scream – Emily was leaning in the basket and making friendly noises to something tiny, black and wriggly: an earwig!

'Can I talk to Mum, anyway?'

'I think she's gone upstairs now. Hang on.'

I dropped the phone, darted over to Emily, moved the log basket behind the settee out of her way and called up the stairs, 'Mum! Helen's on the phone!' After that I dashed up the stairs and shouted down in a muffled, Mum sort of voice, 'Sorry, dear, I'm busy having a shower. Tell her everything's fine and to have a lovely day . . .'

I ran down again. 'Did you hear that?' I said breathlessly. 'Mum's in the shower and said to have a lovely day.'

'I heard . . .' she said suspiciously. 'What's she in the shower for at this time of the morning?'

'She . . . er . . . agghh . . . earwig!' While I'd been running up and down the stairs Emily had squeezed herself behind the settee and somehow got a small log out of the basket with an earwig on it. As I watched, horrified, she popped the earwig into her mouth.

'What?' Helen said in an irritable way. 'What earwig? What are you talking about?'

'An earwig ran on to Mum and she felt she had to have a shower. You know what she's like,' I said faintly, watching Emily's plump cheeks move as she chewed.

'Well, I'll ring later.'

'Don't bother,' I said brightly — or as brightly as I could while watching a baby chewing an earwig. 'Have a lovely time and don't worry about a thing!'

chapter three

'Now,' I said firmly to Emily. 'I'll tidy you up and then you can just sit quietly, looking clean, until Mrs Bayleaf comes.'

I gave a sudden inward shriek of alarm. How could she come? I mean, I couldn't let Mrs Bayleaf know we were on our own – she'd raise the roof, call the authorities, kick up a stink with Mum and Helen. I pondered deeply . . . No, when she arrived I'd have to pretend that Mum had taken Emily out walkies somewhere – and just hope like mad that she didn't want to hang around until they came back. If she did, she'd have a long wait.

In the meantime . . . my eyes shot round into the kitchen – Emily, doing her strange sort of bottom-shuffle and still clutching the log, had moved towards the food cupboards and was now banging them with a chubby hand.

'No, you can't go in those,' I said firmly. I looked at her: the angel top, as well as having bits of egg, butter and a green streak on it, was now covered in sawdusty bits from the log. 'You'll have to come up and sit quietly in your high chair!' I said. 'We're going to the photographer's this afternoon and you've got to look nice and clean.'

She gave a little shriek of protest as I strapped her into her chair. 'Yes,' I said, 'I know it's ridiculous looking clean all the time, but that's what they expect. Never mind; when you're as big as me you can have a nice grubby tracksuit and stay in it all day.'

I took hold of the log firmly. 'Now, the first thing to do is get rid of this dirty old log and give you a . . . a teddy!' I said, spying one sitting on a chair and springing it in front of her. I removed the log but Emily let out a sharp scream and held out her arms for it.

'No. Log is nasty. Dirty,' I said firmly. 'Teddy . . .' I held teddy in front of my face and pretended to kiss him. 'Teddy is lovely.' I made lavish cuddling and kissing gestures. 'Lovely soft fluffy teddy!' I said, making it dance in front of her. I

then held the log at arm's length and looked at it in horror. 'Nasty dirty log!'

Emily took Teddy and dropped him face down into a puddle of milk, then wailed and stretched out her arms for the log.

'But it's a horrible log,' I said. She wailed harder. 'A nasty dirty . . .' But I could see it was useless. I gave in and handed the log back and the wails stopped immediately. She clasped it in her arms and cuddled it. I grinned to myself, remembering Mum telling me that when I'd been small I wouldn't go to sleep unless an umbrella with a duck on its handle was put in my cot with me.

I cleared the table of breakfast things and began to wash up, Emily babbling 'Da-da . . . da-da . . .' to the log as I worked. It did look a bit like Christopher, I thought: pale and wooden.

Once the kitchen was a bit tidy, I went into the bathroom to get a white flannel, wanting to have another go at cleaning Emily. Mum had particularly wanted her to be photographed in the angel top, even though I'd protested that it was much too girlie and frilly. There was even a matching pink-and-white bow to be put in what was nearly a lock of hair on top of her head.

'You'll have to put . . . er . . . Loggy down while I clean you,' I said. Emily wouldn't be parted from him, though, so I had to play a game in which first Emily had her face washed, then it was Loggy's turn.

We were just getting to the rest of Loggy ('And then let's make Loggy's back nice and clean!') when the phone rang. In case Emily tried to escape from the high chair and fell, I took her out and sat her on the floor. Released, she immediately scudded across towards the kitchen cupboards, Loggy under her arm.

I went into the hall — it was Mum again.

'I'm phoning from the train!' she said. 'I explained to this nice young man that it was very urgent and asked if I could use his mobile.'

'Oh yes,' I said, looking nervously after Emily. 'What d'you want this time?'

'Has Helen phoned?'

'Of course she has.'

'And she's on her way home, is she?'

'That's right,' I said. Well, she was. She was going for lunch somewhere and to a stately home on the way, mind you, but Mum hadn't asked *when* she was coming home.

'Oh, thank goodness for that,' Mum said. 'You didn't worry her too much about Gran, did you?'

'No, not at all,' I said truthfully.

'Well, the two of them shouldn't be long getting to you. Are you managing all right in the meantime?'

'Perfectly all right,' I said, straining to see over the kitchen table. 'Looking after babies? Nothing to it!'

'Ha!' Mum said. 'Well, I'd better go, darling. I'll ring from the hospital.'

'OK, Mum,' I said. As I moved into the hall to put the phone back there was a squeaky cupboard-opening noise from the kitchen, then a strange soft plopping, then the sound of a tin hitting the floor. *Emily was in the food cupboard.* 'Must go!' I said.

'Katie! What's happening?' I heard Mum ask frantically just before I dropped the receiver back on to its cradle.

I dashed into the kitchen, and then I screamed. One of the bottom cupboards was open and Emily was sitting beside it, smacking her lips. A tin lay beside her, and on her hair, down her face and coating the pink-and-white angel top was a sticky waterfall of golden syrup.

I stood there in shock for a moment or two, and then I grabbed a newspaper, rushed at her and tried to wipe it off. I dabbed at her and she, copying me, dabbed fondly at the log. Every so often she put sticky newspaper-and-syrup fingers into her mouth and made appreciative noises.

The actual clean-up exercise didn't work too well because the newspaper tore, and the print ran, so that when I'd got the worst of the stickiness off there were black print marks all over her and she had striped syrup-and-print legs. I looked at her in horror. Mum was always going on about *my* appearance but she looked worse than I'd *ever* looked.

'I'll have to bath you!' I wailed, and she beamed at me – I knew she liked a bath. She patted the log. 'Yes, and Loggy,' I said resignedly. I'd have to put them in the bath, and wash the angel top, and just hope it was dry again by the afternoon.

I picked up both her and Loggy to take them to the bathroom, but as I did so there was a ring at the doorbell.

'Coo-ee!' I heard Mrs Bayleaf call through the letter box. 'Only me!'

Only her! I peered round the door and stared at the vast pink shape which had materialised on the other side of the glass front door and, for the second time in five minutes, stood frozen with horror. I didn't intend letting her know I was minding Emily on my own, anyway – but if she saw what a state she was in, I'd get murdered.

There was nothing else to do but run. I wrenched open the back door and rushed into the garden, carrying Emily and Loggy – and then I had an idea. Outside, on the other side of the low wall to Laura-next-door's garden, was an old pram which Laura used to put Jamie in when he slept outside. Desperate now, I reached over and plonked Emily in it, remembering to do up the harness so she couldn't fall out. This done, I ran back in the house.

'Helloooo! Is there anybody there?' Mrs Bayleaf

was now calling rather desperately through the letter box.

Well, there was nothing else for it: someone that size wasn't going to go away. I dropped a washing-up bowl over the mess of syrup and newspaper on the floor of the kitchen, took a deep breath and went to answer the door.

chapter four

Plastering a smile on my face, I opened up.

'Where is the little angel, then?' Mrs Bayleaf gushed. 'Where is the little boofums bunny?'

Before I could turn her away at the door by pretending we'd all got bubonic plague, she was in. Crumbs, she looked ghastly – she was wearing a power-woman outfit from the eighties or something: a suit in a pink so bright it hurt your eyes, with shoulders wide enough to get you turfed off a bus. Round her neck hung half of Harrods' jewellery counter. Half woman, half pink mountain, she steamrollered her way down the hall, glanced in each room, peered into corners, looked behind doors.

She paused in the kitchen, turning to me in anguish. 'But where is the treasure, the sweetest lambkin?'

'Out,' I said.

'*Out?!*' Her vast powdered face crumbled, her shoulder pads heaved. It was not a pretty sight. 'But surely . . .'

'Mum's terribly sorry,' I said, thinking I'd better make it sound good, 'but she had to go out unexpectedly. Something to do with Gran. Very urgent. She said she felt awful about letting you down but there was nothing she could do.'

'But I had the morning off specially from the store. I haven't seen little Emily for a month, you know. Babies change so much.'

'Yes, I suppose they do,' I said politely.

'I remember my Christopher. He was the sweetest little boy with grey flannel trousers and a runny nose – and then one day I turned round and he was a man.'

Oh yes, I thought. A likely tale.

She paused by the back door, gazing out into the garden. 'Oh well, I suppose I might just as well go into work, after all. After Six Cocktail and Continental Cruise Wear comes to a full stop without me, you know.'

'I'm sure they'll be really pleased to see you,' I lied, thinking that Bliss's department store was probably hanging flags out to mark her absence.

She suddenly fixed her gaze on next-door's pram with this-door's baby sitting in it.

'I didn't know you had . . .' her voice lowered to a horrified whisper, '. . . *New Age travellers next door*.' She craned her head in order to see better; the gold chains round her neck clanked. 'There's a perfectly ghastly baby out there in a pram. Absolutely filthy, wearing rags.'

'Er . . . is there?' I said faintly.

She sighed with disgust. 'What is the neighbourhood coming to? The child looks neglected.

Should I call the authorities, do you think? Do Social Services know there's a derelict baby in the area?'

I made a vague sort of 'don't know' noise.

She looked again. 'And . . . are my eyes deceiving me? I do believe the child is playing with a log!'

'Never!'

She stood in the doorway, wringing her hands. 'When I think of all the beautiful toys our little Emily has, I could weep. To think that a child is reduced to playing with a *log*.'

She shook her head sadly. 'My Cedric would say I shouldn't interfere — but promise me that you'll never let our babykins play with that child in that pram!'

I nodded solemnly. 'I promise.'

She looked at the pram and her shoulders heaved. 'Such a poor, poor child. So disadvantaged, so plain. And our poppety darling so beautiful . . .'

I fixed her with a glassy smile.

'Still, there you are. We can't all have the advantage of good-looking parents, can we?'

Before I could say anything about this she moved into the hall, looking at her watch. 'I may as well be getting to work; I don't want to waste the morning.'

She paused at the front door. 'Tell your mother I came, will you? Beattie and Cedric send their love.' I opened the door for her and she levered her way out and steamed down the garden path. 'And a big kissy-boo for the rosebud!'

'Of course,' I said with dignity.

At the gate – just as I was about to slam the door and sigh with relief – she turned, waving a Bliss's carrier bag. 'Oh! I almost forgot!'

I'd noticed the bag but because, as far as I was concerned, nothing good had ever come from Mrs Bayleaf or her department store – and because I was scared it was some sort of revolting outfit for me – I'd decided not to mention it in the hopes it would go away.

It wasn't for me, though.

'Now, your mother told me she was planning a little surprise for Helen . . . a photographic sur-prise!' she said. 'And I thought that my part of the surprise could be a dress for our darling!'

I brightened slightly. Maybe Mrs Bayleaf had at last come up trumps, because a new dress, a clean dress, was just what we could do with. Even if I could wash all the syrup and log off the pink and white thing, I bet it would never be dry in time for her to wear to the photographer's.

'This baby dress,' she said coyly, 'is a rather special one.' She rustled the bag. 'I got my bridal department to run it up from some spare material in . . . guess what colour?'

'Not . . . not whisper blue?' I said faintly.

'With exquisite beading!' she added in triumph.

She held up the small dress with its bows and frills and twiddly bits and all my worst brides-maidly nightmares came back to me. *Whisper blue with exquisite beading* ... I'd hoped never to hear those words again.

'She'll look a picture in that!' said Mrs Bayleaf.

Just then, Laura-next-door came out of her front door to collect the milk from the step.

'Morning!' she said to the two of us. 'Lovely day!'

Mrs Bayleaf looked at her sternly. 'It is for some,' she said, steam almost rising from her words. 'Those that don't neglect their children, for instance.'

Laura's smile faded.

'If some mothers just occasionally used a bar of soap, it might help.' Mrs Bayleaf closed the garden gate with a loud, disapproving bang. 'Goodbye, Katie. Love to your mother!' she called over her shoulder as she sailed off down the road.

'Well!' Laura said. 'Who's that old trout?'

'Never seen her before in my life,' I said, and then I galloped through into the back garden to get Emily out of Jamie's pram before anyone else saw her.

chapter five

I'd got Emily in and was gathering things ready for the bath when the front doorbell rang again. I peered round the corner of the kitchen in case Mrs Bayleaf had come back, but as a vast pink mountain hadn't formed on the other side of the front door, it seemed safe to answer it.

'Crumbs,' Flicka said as soon as I opened the door. 'Is that the baby?' She stood back, aghast. 'What've you done to her?'

I held Emily at arm's length and looked at her. 'She's not that bad, is she?'

Flicka nodded. 'Worse. She's all sticky — and why does it say *POLICE* in backwards newsprint on her forehead?'

'It's a long story,' I said, 'but basically she's managed to get scrambled egg and a bit of bread and half a tin of syrup and some newspaper on her.'

'And some leaves from the garden,' Flicka said, picking one out of Emily's hair. 'And what's this in her hand?'

'Ugh!' She picked it out and dropped it in disgust. 'A caterpillar!'

We stared at the floor. 'No, worse than that,' I said. 'Half a caterpillar.'

'What's happened to the other half?'

'She must have eaten it,' I said. 'She's very fond of wildlife.'

'But how did she get like that?' Flicka asked, still looking slightly dazed. 'And why's she carrying a bit of wood?'

'That's not just a piece of wood,' I said. 'That's her friend Loggy.'

Flicka rolled her eyes. 'Doesn't your mum mind her looking like this?'

I shifted Emily from one hip to the other. 'That's just it,' I said. 'Mum's not here right now.' And I explained about Gran and about Helen – and about me knowing that I could cope perfectly well on my own.

'And I *can* cope,' I said. 'It's just that things keep happening. But now you're here I'm going to clean her up and put her in Mrs Bayleaf's dress and then you can help me get her to the photographer's.'

'Oh. Right,' Flicka said nervously.

I gave Flicka a friendly punch. 'You know about these things – you've got a little sister, haven't you? And two of us can manage one small baby!'

'I s'pose we can,' Flicka said doubtfully as we went off to the bathroom.

'So what do we do next?' I asked, once we had two inches of lukewarm water in the bath. Emily gurgled happily and I lifted her high in the air.

'Just dump her in?'

'I think you ought to take her clothes off first,' Flicka said.

'But this will be much quicker and then I won't have —'

Flicka tutted, sounding just like Mum. 'Could *you* have a proper wash with all your clothes on?'

I nodded. 'I often do.'

'But then you haven't poured golden syrup all over yourself,' she pointed out.

'That's true.'

Together we got Emily's clothes off. It was

harder than it sounds, because the golden syrup had stuck her vest to her dress, but we managed it in the end without too much yelling.

'I don't know what you're going to do about her hair,' Flicka said, looking at the sticky mess on Emily's head. 'They hate their hair being washed. My little sister just used to scream and scream . . .'

I pulled a face. 'Just my luck that she'll be yelling her head off and Helen will phone –'

'Oggy!' Emily said suddenly, and Flicka and I looked at each other.

'What?' we said together.

'Does she mean . . . *log*, d'you think?' Flicka asked.

I nodded excitedly. 'That's two words she can say! Helen will be really excited.'

'I shouldn't be too sure,' Flicka said. 'People are pleased when babies say Mummy and Daddy and Granny and all that – I don't know about Loggy.'

'Oggy!' Emily said again, pointing to Loggy on the side of the bath.

'You can't have him in the bath,' I said, and Emily's face crumpled. She stretched forward, made a wild grab for Loggy and he fell in, taking a tube of toothpaste and a big plastic bottle of bubble bath with him.

'Quick! Loggy's drowning!' Flicka said.

'Never mind him,' I said. 'Look at the bubble bath!'

I'd used it that morning, so naturally it didn't have its top on, and the slimy pink liquid was glugging out into the water. It was a giant bottle of Mum's, and once it was out there seemed almost as much of it as there was bath water.

I made a few attempts to scoop it back into the

bottle but only succeeding in making bubbles. Emily, fascinated, patted the water and, as she patted, more bubbles appeared. We all swished it around and soon Emily had almost disappeared under a froth of white. Delighted, she threw handfuls of foam everywhere.

'This is never going to go away!' I said. 'It's like in the cartoons: the bubbles will go down the stairs and fill up the entire house and then we go floating out and –'

'Never mind all that,' Flicka said. 'We can wash her hair with it!'

So we did that as best we could and got nearly all the newsprint off too, and, after Loggy was cleaned up, they both looked much better. Flicka went to get a towel out of the airing cupboard.

'Didn't you get one for Loggy?' I asked when she came back, and she looked at me as if I was mad.

'A bath towel for a piece of wood?'

'Don't talk about him like that,' I said – I was getting quite fond of him. 'Even logs have feelings.'

It took us ages to get Emily into the whisper-blue number – it had hundreds of little covered buttons all down the back, and the puff sleeves were so tight that we could hardly get her arms inside them, but at last we surveyed the finished article. Pink from the bath, cross at being parted from Loggy for so long and stuffed into a round puffball of whisper blue complete with exquisite beading, Emily looked revolting.

'There's something about the clothes that that woman buys,' Flicka said, shaking her head at Emily's appearance. 'D'you think she does it deliberately?'

'Mrs Bayleaf?' I nodded. 'Course she does.'

'At least she's clean, I suppose,' Flicka said. 'And she's wearing the sort of thing they're always photographed in – you know, soppy frills and all that.'

Emily gave a whimper.

'What now?' Flicka asked.

'She wants Loggy to have a dress on?'

Flicka shook her head. 'I expect she's just hungry.'

'Well, there's pizza,' I said. 'And tomato soup for Emily.'

We both looked at Emily and gave a short scream.

'Tomato soup does not go with whisper blue,' I said.

'We shouldn't have put the dress on her yet!'

I thought for a moment. 'I know,' I said. 'Let's put her back in her sleepsuit.'

'We can't undo all those buttons again – she'll scream the place down.'

'We'll put it over the dress – like a huge bib! You get her in it, I'll get the pizza on,' I added, choosing the easy option.

Five minutes later, while I was still busy microwaving, Flicka and Emily appeared. Emily looked very odd – like a small hot air balloon. The sleepsuit was stretched to its limit, bulging and bursting with scrunched-up whisper blue.

'It was a bit difficult doing it up,' Flicka said. 'Not to say exhausting.'

'But now you've got her in it she can stay like that all the way to the photographer's,' I said, 'and she'll be all beautiful and clean for her picture!'

'Let's hope so,' said Flicka doubtfully.

chapter six

'How d'you know when it's cooked?' I asked anxiously, stirring soup.

'Soup doesn't have to be cooked,' Flicka said. 'Just warmed up.'

'But don't you have to put your elbow in it to test it?'

'That's bath water,' she said. 'Come here – I'll finish it.'

We took great care feeding her, but in spite of all our efforts Emily and Loggy got a fair covering of tomato soup. I felt it quite suited Loggy, actually – gave him a bit of colour after his bath – but Emily ended up with a bright orange moustache and beard. Even when we'd wiped it off a faint orangeyness stayed behind.

'I hope that won't come out in the photograph,' I said.

'We'd better take a soap and flannel with us,' Flicka advised. 'That way we can do a last-minute clean-up job.'

After she'd eaten, Emily started getting a bit fidgety, rubbing her eyes and making a funny whining noise. We jollied her about for a while, sitting on the kitchen floor with her playing Hunt the Loggy, but that only seemed to make things worse.

'Did she have a sleep this morning?' Flicka asked, and I clapped my hand to my mouth.

'I forgot all about it!'

'That's it, then. No wonder she's miserable.'

'Anyway,' Flicka said, as Emily suddenly lolled sideways on to a cushion. 'I don't think she's waiting for you to remember to put her in her cot. She's going to sleep now.'

Emily closed her eyes and put her thumb in.

'And now I suppose you'll be saying that the piece of wood wants a nap,' said Flicka.

'Even logs get tired,' I said, tucking Loggy up next to Emily. We put a cot blanket over them both and cushions all round. 'There. Nothing can possibly happen to her there, can it?'

Flicka shook her head. 'She's perfectly safe. She

can fall out of a cot, but she can't fall out of the floor, can she?'

We went out to play on my trampoline, feeling like we'd been let out of school. Every now and then we stopped to look through the window and make sure she was still asleep. Everything was fine and we'd done a fair bit of bouncing and I'd shown off my special backward and sideways flip-flop twists, when I looked at my watch.

'We'd better wake her in ten minutes to give ourselves plenty of time to get to the photographer's,' I said to Flicka – and just then the phone went.

I ran in to answer it, straight through the kitchen to the front hall. As my hand was about to close on the phone, though, I stopped dead: I'd run straight through the kitchen *but Emily hadn't been there*!

Flicka, close behind me, gave a shriek. 'Where's she gone?'

I backtracked and we stared at the cot blanket and pillows. 'She can't be far!' I said. 'You look for her, I'll get the phone.'

It was Helen again. 'I forgot to tell Mum that now Emily's older she sometimes does without an afternoon nap,' she said.

'Oh. Right,' I said distractedly.

'Has she had an afternoon nap?'

'Sort of,' I said.

'Well, has she or hasn't she?' Helen said irrita-
bly – I must say being a mother hadn't exactly
improved her temper. 'Put Mum on, will you? I'll
be able to get some sense out of her.'

'I can tell you!' I said quickly. 'You don't need
to bother Mum. Emily had an afternoon nap, but
it was the morning one running late.'

'Oh,' Helen said.

She sounded odd and suspicious again, so I
quickly added, 'And – guess what? She's said a
new word!'

'Has she really?' said Helen eagerly. 'Was it
"Mummy"?'

'No. "Loggy",' I said.

'Loggy. Doggy, I suppose that means.'

'No, it . . .' but it was too complicated to go
into on the phone. 'Yes, that's right,' I said.

'I don't suppose it's really a word . . .' Helen
said wistfully. 'She's just babbling nonsense.'

'No, it's definitely a word,' I said. 'You should

hear her – clear as a bell!'

'Go on, then – get her to say it now!' Helen said, and too late I realised that I'd dug myself into a hole.

My heart sank. I waved frantically to Flicka, who'd just come up from hunting behind the settee. 'Come and talk to Mummy, Emily!' I said. 'Come and say "Loggy" for Mummy!'

'Do I have to?' Flicka mouthed in disgust, and I nodded emphatically.

'Come along, coochie-woochie bunny!' I cooed.

Flicka gave me an anguished look. I ignored it,

tickled her under the chin and passed her the phone.

'Gug . . . gug . . . Loggy,' she said in a deadpan voice, and I whipped the phone away quickly.

'Hear that?' I said to Helen. 'Marvellous, wasn't it? Clear as anything. Isn't she clever? Got to go now, we're playing Hunt the Emily.'

And in deadly earnest, too . . .

She wasn't behind the settees and she wasn't in the kitchen cupboards or under the tablecloth. I even looked upstairs for her – though I don't know how she'd have been able to get over the stair-gate.

'Oh-oh!' Flicka said, pausing at the bottom of the stairs. 'There's a little bit of chewed wallpaper just here . . . and a small piece of bark.'

Together we whipped open the cupboard under the stairs – and found Emily and Loggy playing with a pile of old, discarded shoes. And something else. As we stared into the darkness I got an awful sinking feeling . . .

'Er . . . what's all that black stuff on her?' Flicka asked.

'I think . . . shoe polish,' I said faintly.

We hauled her out. Loggy was a black loggy now, and Emily was wearing a black sleepsuit and had little black blotchy hands and a stripy face.

We stared at her in horror.

'That won't come off easily,' Flicka said.

'But at least it's not on her dress!' There was a bit of whisper blue peeping out of the gaps between the poppers. 'Not much, anyway,' I added. I looked at my watch again. 'We've got to go! The bus leaves from the end of the road at a quarter to.'

I shoved Emily at Flicka. 'I'll get the soap and

flannel and stuff and we'll clean her up when we get there!' I shouted as I raced upstairs.

I tore down again, stuffing things into a bag. 'Loggy's covered in shoe polish so we'll have to try and leave him here,' I said. 'I'll get the buggy out while you distract her.'

Unfortunately, Emily wouldn't be distracted. She'd go into the buggy all right, but she wouldn't be parted from Loggy.

'We'll have to take him,' I said.

'It's not a him, it's an it,' Flicka said.

I ignored her. 'I wonder if Laura would lend us

her double buggy . . .'

'If you think,' Flicka said, 'that I'm walking down the road with a baby covered in boot polish sitting in one seat and a piece of wood sitting in the other, you can think again.'

'OK, OK, keep your hair on!'

Together we wriggled the buggy out of the door.

'Hang on!' I said suddenly. 'I'm not even sure where the studio is. I'll get the appointment card.'

I found it and then had another small fit.

'You won't believe this!' I groaned. 'The photographer's studio is in Bliss's. If Mrs Bayleaf sees us we're dead . . .'

chapter seven

As we galloped down the road I looked over my shoulder and saw the bus coming round the corner.

'Quick! We mustn't miss it!' I said to Flicka, and as we arrived, panting, at the bus stop, I whipped Emily out of the buggy and grabbed up

Loggy and the bag of washing stuff. I passed the buggy to Flicka. 'D'you know how to fold these up?'

'No idea,' she said as the bus drew up alongside us. 'I think it's . . . ow!' She pulled her hand out quickly and sucked her finger.

'Perhaps it's . . . ow . . . ow!' I said, as (a) Emily dropped Loggy on my foot and (b) a metal catch at the top of the buggy deliberately bit me.

'I think you're supposed to wiggle this,' Flicka said. She pulled a lever on the buggy and it promptly crumpled to the ground, making us jump back. We stared at it nervously, as if it might leap up and attack us at any time.

'Are you coming on this bus or did you just stop me to admire its paintwork?' the driver called through the open door.

Biting back a sarcastic comment – if he drove off and left us we wouldn't get to the photographer's on time – we climbed aboard and paid our fares.

'Now,' I said as we collapsed into our seats, 'have we got everything?' I ticked off on my fingers: 'Emily's hairbrush and the bow for her hair and clean socks and two flannels and soap and . . .'

There was a sudden cry of 'Oggy!' from Emily, and I froze for a moment and then suddenly sprung into action.

'Stop that bus!' I called to the driver. He was counting out money and hadn't actually started it yet, but I do like to get the full drama out of everything.

'What is it?' he said, looking round. 'Forget the kitchen sink?' And he laughed hugely at his joke.

'Could you just open the front door again, please?' I said, passing Emily to Flicka and getting up. 'The baby's dropped her log on the pavement.'

He raised one eyebrow. 'Dropped her dog?' he said. 'You want to watch out you girls don't get reported. A baby shouldn't be in charge of a dog. A dog could quite easily break a leg if it was dropped. A dog —'

'No. A *log*,' I said.

'Besides, dogs aren't allowed on these buses. Only guide dogs.' He raised one eyebrow and looked at me severely. 'Is yours a guide dog?'

I jumped off swiftly, retrieved Loggy and

showed it to him. 'This is a *log*,' I said. I smiled politely. 'If it makes you feel happier, we can refer to it as a guide log though.'

'Don't you get lippy with me, young lady,' he said, starting up the bus.

I sat down and Emily clutched Loggy to her fondly, making kissing noises. Flicka looked at them and shook her head. 'I don't know how you're going to break it to Helen that that old stick is now a member of the family,' she said.

Getting off at the bus station in town, we managed to get the buggy up and working again without too many squashed fingers. We set off at a fair pace for Bliss's, wheeling past shops and round people as quickly as we could.

After a while, Flicka said, 'Have you noticed how everyone keeps looking at us?'

I shook my head.

'Well, looking at Emily, really.'

'People always do look at babies,' I explained. 'They look at them and then they smile in a soppy coochie-coo way.'

'They're not exactly doing that,' she said. 'It's more a look of astonishment. Well, just look at

her reflection in the mirror in this window.'

We looked. The grey-and-black sleepsuit was bulging everywhere, but mostly around Emily's tummy, so that it looked as if she had a basket of fruit under her vest. Where the poppers of the suit gaped, chunks of whisper blue showed through, and most of those chunks now had smears of shoe polish on them. Her face was smudged with black all over – like those pictures of little boy sweeps that you see in the history books – and in her arms she clutched a log.

'See what I mean?' Flicka said. 'She's not exactly your bonny baby food advertisement, is she?'

'Never mind,' I said. 'We'll fix her up as soon as we get to the photographer's – they're bound to have a washroom. Just as long as we don't see anyone we know, we'll be all right . . .' And we looked around us fearfully, for we were fast approaching Bliss's.

We arrived at the big glass doors at the front and a woman, coming out, held them open for us. As we passed through, her jaw dropped and she stared after us as if we were a circus act.

'Just ignore her,' I muttered to Flicka.

'Now, all we've got to do is stay away from After Six Cocktail and Continental Cruise Wear on the fifth,' Flicka said. 'What floor is the photographer on?'

I dug out his card and looked at it. 'The fifth . . .'

Flicka gave a sharp scream.

'It's not *that* bad,' I said. 'You can go first and spy out where the studio is and then I'll dash . . .'

'No — it's too late!' Flicka said in a strangled voice. 'Auntie Beattie Bayleaf is coming . . . striding straight towards us, looking like a pink army tank!'

I shoved the buggy at Flicka. 'Don't just stand there, then — go!' I said. 'Meet you somewhere later.'

They disappeared into the crowd and I composed my face: changed the frantic, anguished look to one of pleasant surprise.

'Oh! Mrs Bailey!' I said. 'Fancy seeing you here.'

'I work here, Katie, dear. But what are you . . .' Her face powder suddenly creased into a large smile as she spotted the baby in the pushchair just behind us. 'Oh! Darling possums!'

The baby was about Emily's age, I suppose, and its mother, draped in a white plastic cape, was having her eyes made up behind the nearby beauty counter.

Mrs Bayleaf bent down so that her face was inches from the baby's. It was asleep, luckily, or the shock could have been fatal. 'What a little angel it is!' she breathed on it. 'Look at that forehead — so like my Christopher's — means she's going to be terribly brainy. And that darling nose . . . those eyelashes . . . that rosebud mouth . . .'

I coughed long and loudly to try to distract her — at this rate she was going to open its mouth in a minute to look at its teeth.

'Are you all right, Katie?' she asked, straightening up.

'Bad cough . . .' I said, thumping my chest.

'And where's your mother?'

'She's . . . er . . . talking,' I said. I crossed my fingers. 'We've come in to have the photographs taken. Mum's meeting me there — at the studio.'

'But why isn't Emily wearing my beautiful dress?'

'We're keeping it clean for the photograph,' I

said. 'And I really ought to be off there now . . .'

She put her hand on the pushchair. 'I'll come with you, dear. Then I can have a chat to your mother about that deprived child who lives next door to you.'

'No!'

'What?'

'I . . . er . . .' I searched my mind frantically. 'I just remembered – I told Mum I'd meet her here, not there, and she'll be very cross if we just disappear. She might be ages and ages. She said she probably would be ages and ages.'

Mrs Bayleaf searched the crowd as if looking for Mum, but gave up after a few moments. 'Perhaps I'd better not wait,' she said, and I nearly passed out with relief. 'After Six Cocktail and Continental Cruise Wear is very short-staffed at the moment. Do come and see me afterwards, though,' she added. 'I've some marvellously trendy items going in my sale – just suit a fab young thing like you!'

'I'm not sure if we'll have time . . .' I said.

She patted the baby's head. 'Sweet, sweet thing,' she cooed.

As she sailed off into the distance, the baby's mother dived off her stool and came towards us, cape flying, eyes newly made up in parrot green.

'What a cheek!' she said, glowering after Mrs Bayleaf. 'Touching my baby!'

I joined her in a glower. 'Some people have got a real nerve, haven't they?' I said indignantly.

'They lock up Rottweilers – they ought to lock up women like that!' she said. 'Mauling my baby, patting it, frightening it to death. Who *was* she?'

'Don't know – but I'll certainly give evidence against her,' I said. 'She shouldn't be allowed.'

chapter eight

We arrived at the photographer's studio out of
breath and all of a bundle. Getting there had been
like a spy film: we'd gone to the fifth floor by lift,
then, while I'd flattened myself against the lift
walls, Flicka had peered out and made sure the
coast was clear of Mrs Bayleaf. We'd then done a

mad buggy-charge across the shop floor and skid-
ded to a halt just by the studio reception desk and
the sign which said: *'Immortalise your baby's most
beautiful days!'*

The receptionist's jaw dropped. For some
moments she stared at us and we stared back at
her, then she remembered her manners.

'Er . . . can I help you?' she asked faintly. She
was blonde, frizzy-haired and looked even glossier
than the women you get on the make-up counters.

'Yes, please,' I said. 'We've an appointment at
three-thirty to have Emily's photograph taken.
Full studio sitting and six mounted portraits.'

Glossy stood up and peered over her desk at us,
and Emily and Loggy peered back at her with
little boot-black faces. For some moments the
receptionist didn't say anything; I suppose she was
taking in Emily's generous plastering of shoe-
polish, the faint trace of tomato moustache on her
top lip and her general balloon-like appearance.
'Is *this* Emily?' she asked, not even trying to con-
ceal the horror in her voice.

'It certainly is,' I said. 'Emily with Loggy. And
if you'll kindly direct us to your washroom we'll

get her ready. She doesn't normally look like this.'

'I'm glad to hear it,' Glossy said, pursing silvery pink lips. She led us behind the counter and through to an inner room. It was hushed, quiet, with white walls and pale pink carpet. Photographs of babies hung on the walls in ornate gold frames, and there were fluffy teddies and bunnies sitting on silk armchairs.

'If you'd wait here . . .' Glossy said in a pained voice, and disappeared round a corner deeper in.

Flicka and I looked at the babies in the photographs. They all seemed to have starchy white dresses or starchy blue shirts, their hair was shiny and their faces beamed with health. Each sat on a furry rug, clutching something small and fluffy and smiling a fat and toothless smile at the camera.

'Crumbs,' Flicka said. 'Emily doesn't look like any of those. They're all clean and posh.'

'That's all right,' I said cheerfully. 'Emily will be clean and posh in a minute – we've just got to get her out of that sleepsuit and give her a quick once-over with a flannel.'

'Mmm,' Flicka said, looking at the photographs on the wall and then back to Emily doubtfully.

She moved towards a blue silk armchair and then hesitated. 'I'm scared to sit down in here.'

I looked at my grubby trainers and then at the pale pink carpet. 'I'm scared to stand up.'

While we hesitated and hovered, feeling as out of place as a butcher at a vegetarian party, we heard voices from the inner sanctum and Glossy and a woman wearing dungarees came round the corner. The dungaree woman was the photographer – I knew that because she had a load of things hanging round her neck.

'See what I mean . . .' Glossy said in a low voice to the photographer, but the photographer just looked at us and smiled broadly.

She crouched down and spoke to Emily. 'What a marvellous-looking baby!' she said. 'Full of character.'

'Yes, and we can get her looking posh,' I said. 'We just need two minutes and a washroom. She's got her best dress under that sleepsuit and we'll try to get Loggy off her and make her play with a teddy . . .'

'So this is her friend Loggy, is it?' the photographer asked.

'She has *got* teddies,' Flicka put in desperately. 'Loads of them. Hundreds . . .'

'But she prefers a piece of wood.' The photographer stood up and stared at Emily. 'If you only knew how refreshing this baby is! I take pictures of babies all day: overfed, shiny, new-pin clean babies – and I'm sick to death of them. Sometimes I long for a grubby, scruffy baby with a runny nose.'

'Her nose does run if she cries,' I put in.

'A baby who looks as if she's allowed to be

herself,' the photographer went on enthusiastically. 'A baby who isn't just a fashion accessory.'

'Humph,' Glossy said, and she sniffed disapprovingly and went back to her desk.

The photographer unclipped Emily from her buggy and put her on the floor. Emily immediately started scuffling along the carpet on her bottom, Loggy clutched firmly in one arm. She made for a wicker wastepaper basket and turned it over, scattering pieces of paper everywhere, patting them across the floor.

'Oops,' I said, making for her.

'No. Leave her.' The photographer looked at her for some time and then said, 'Look, if you don't mind, I'd like to take some photographs of Emily just as she is. We'll get her out of that ghastly lump of a dress she's wearing under the sleepsuit and maybe take some shots just wearing a vest and nappy.'

'But . . . why?' I asked in confusion.

'Well, I've got this commission from one of the colour supplements of a Sunday newspaper,' she went on. 'I'm presenting a series of photographs of children – soft focus, idealised shots, and I'd like to contrast them with some photos of what a real baby would look like – and the sort of thing it would play with – if left to its own devices.'

'Um . . . well . . .' I said, wondering what Mum and Helen would have to say about it.

She clapped her hands excitedly. 'Just think – Emily on the cover with grubby face, filthy vest, runny nose, clutching a log!'

'Er . . .' I said, and I knew Mum and Helen wouldn't bother to say anything to me, they'd just kill me where I stood.

'Emily's photograph – nationwide!' said the photographer enthusiastically.

'Emily's auntie – dead,' I said.

'Oh, come. I'm sure when Emily's mother learns how much money she could earn she'll be happy. There'll be enough to keep Emily in logs for life!'

'I don't know . . .' I said, watching Emily eating an envelope.

'They'll murder you,' put in Flicka. 'And me as well.'

'Maybe they won't recognise her,' I said.

The photographer smiled at me. 'Maybe we could even have a small photo of you in the magazine, holding Emily.'

Well, that was the decider. 'Done!' I said.

Emily didn't look much better out of the sleep-suit and the whisper-blue number, because the shoe polish had found its way right down to her vest and a knot of golden syrup was discovered still lurking in her hair. The photographer wouldn't let us do a thing to change her, though – except get her to cry so her nose would run. We did this by taking Loggy away for half a minute.

'Gorgeous! Utterly natural!' the photographer enthused as she clicked away, but Glossy took one

look, shuddered and asked if she could leave early.

We didn't have to worry about seeing Mrs Bayleaf on the way out, because by the time about four hundred photographs had been taken from every angle you could think of, the store was closed. The photographer said she'd be in touch on Monday and thanked us *very* much for coming.

Flicka was all for cleaning up Emily before we set off home.

'Just in case anyone sees us,' she said anxiously.

I said I couldn't be bothered, though, and just stuck her back in the sleepsuit. 'It's not worth it,'

I said. 'We'll be home ages before anyone else, so we can give her a bath and get her into clean night things and put her to bed and no one will be any the wiser.'

'What about when they see the photographs, though?' Flicka asked fearfully.

'Oh, that'll be OK,' I said. 'I'll let them know about them gradually. First I'll impress everyone with the wonderful job I've made of looking after Emily today, show them how clean and well cared-for she is, and then I'll slowly bring up the subject of the photographs. I'll sort of infer that they're for the cover of *Vogue*.'

'I see,' Flicka said. 'And gradually let them find out that the photographs are actually to contrast some beautiful clean babies with a dirty one?'

'A *natural* one,' I corrected her.

Everyone stared at us on the bus again, but I was getting used to it. Walking back to our house, Emily sucked her thumb and then fell asleep; a line of dribble ran down her chin and left a white path behind it through the grime.

'Look at that,' I said. 'Pity the photographer can't see it. Artistic, that is. Well worth a few photographs.'

But Flicka wasn't listening. Flicka was clutching my arm, nodding towards our house and making whimpering noises. 'Look — t-two cars outside,' she said, pointing with a shaking hand.

'That's right — one's Mum's and one's Helen's,' I said. 'They're both back.' I suddenly realised what I'd said and shrieked in horror. *They're both back!'*

We stood at the end of our road as if turned to stone.

'Wh . . . what shall we do now?' Flicka asked.

'There's n-nothing *to* do,' I quivered, staring at

the cars hard and wishing I had magic powers to make them disappear. 'We've just got to go back and face the music.'

Flicka started piling bits and pieces into my arms. 'Nearly right – except for the "we" bit,' she said. '*You've* got to go back and face the music.'

'But . . . but . . .'

'Urgent appointment elsewhere,' she said, tucking a flannel under my arm and popping half a jar of baby food into my jacket pocket. 'Good luck and everything. Let me know when you get out.'

I stared at her, clutched her arm. 'Oh, come on!' I said. 'You wouldn't just go off and leave a friend, would you?'

'Goodbye,' she said.

chapter nine

'Come back!' I yelled after her, but she'd already disappeared round the corner back to the bus stop.

I hesitated for a moment, wondering about emigrating to Australia or running away to sea, but decided I'd left it too late. I took a deep breath and carried on pushing the buggy slowly towards home.

When I got near the house I could see Mrs Bayleaf, Helen, Christopher and Mum with the net curtains pulled aside, all looking out of the front window. When they spotted me, their mouths all opened together and they pointed at me and then at Emily, looking relieved, outraged, furious and *just-wait-till-I-get-hold-of-you*-ish in turn. By the time I got to the top of the path they were out of the door and all round me, doing a war-dance.

'Wherever have you *been*?'

'How *could* you?'

'I never would have believed it!'

'We were just about to call the police!'

Everyone said all the above at least three times, and then Mrs Bayleaf sort of reeled backwards, clutching her forehead. 'But that . . . that's the New Age baby you've got there!' she said. 'That's the awful, dirty little baby next door.'

'Do you mind!' Helen said indignantly, undoing the strap and whipping Emily out of the buggy in one swift movement. 'This is my Emily.'

She glowered at Mrs Bayleaf. Mrs Bayleaf glowered back. Emily woke up and, because Helen hadn't picked up Loggy, began to scream.

'What have you *done* to her!' Helen said to me in an outraged voice.

Mum looked around nervously; curtains were beginning to twitch on all sides. 'Perhaps we'd better all go inside and calm down a little and then Katie can tell us what she's been doing,' she said.

We went inside the house. Not very far inside – just as far as the hall. Here they ranged themselves around me, positioned on stairs and in doorways – there seemed an awful lot of them. Emily carried on screaming.

'She wants her log,' I said to Helen.

'Don't you tell me what she wants!' Helen said, still outraged, then, as the screaming continued, '*What?*'

'Her log,' I said. 'It's in the buggy.'

'*Log!*' Helen said. 'She doesn't want a log – not when she's got beautiful hand-crafted educational toys.'

'It'll stop her crying,' I said. 'And then you'll all

be able to have a *real* go at me. At the moment I can't quite hear what you're shouting.'

The log was brought in. Emily stopped yelling and started smiling.

'You see,' I said quietly and reasonably, 'she's perfectly all right. At the moment she just . . . just looks a bit different, that's all.'

'Different!'

'Filthy, you mean!'

'Disgusting!'

'Revolting!'

'New Age!' Mrs Bayleaf said daringly.

'Look,' I said, even more quietly and reasonably. 'I can explain . . .'

'Make it good,' Christopher said between gritted teeth.

So I told them everything — about wanting Helen and Christopher to have a proper anniversary weekend, and imitating Mum on the phone, and trying to stop Emily from getting dirty and not having much success, and then having to pretend she lived next door, and then about the shoe polish. I was just getting round to the photographer bit when Mrs Bayleaf found the whisper-blue

number screwed up in the bottom of the buggy. It had been trailing along the floor and Flicka had tripped on it once, so it didn't look too good.

'This is never the beautiful little frock I had made!' she said in a horrified voice, holding up something very like the rag Dad uses to clean the car.

'Yes . . . well . . . er . . .' I said. 'We were trying to keep it clean for the photographs but it got a bit of shoe polish on, and then it got a bit screwed up and then Flicka stood . . .'

'Katie!' Mum interrupted in a deeply terrifying voice. 'Don't tell me you've had Emily's photograph taken! Please don't tell me you've had her photograph taken *looking like that*!'

The four faces loomed at me again. 'Well, that's the next thing,' I said nervously. 'In a manner of speaking, not to put too fine a point upon it, I . . . er . . .'

'Upstairs!' Mum said. 'Up to your room straightaway while we decide what to do with you. As it is I feel just *too* furious to speak to you a moment longer.'

I stumped upstairs slowly and crossly and flung

myself on my bed. Downstairs, I could hear a sort of continuous mumble of '*I would never have believed it of her . . . Absolutely neglected . . . Never seen Emily in such a state . . . In my opinion, just like a New Age baby.*'

About fifteen minutes later there was the noise of a car outside, and then a knock at the door. I crept to the top of the stairs; knowing my luck it would probably be the bus driver coming to complain about me, or someone who'd seen us in the street wanting another look.

It wasn't either, though; it was the photographer from the studio. She came into the hall and then there was a muddled conversation between everyone about who she was and who *they* all were, then I heard her say, 'I've rush-printed some of the photographs I took of Emily and I simply had to come round.'

'Just let me explain . . .' Helen began.

'She doesn't normally look like this . . .' Christopher put in.

Mum coughed. 'Just at this moment, of course, she looks absolutely appalling, but . . .'

'I mean, who could *blame* me for thinking she

was a New Age baby . . .'

'No – please don't apologise!' the photographer said. 'I think Emily's absolutely terrific. Very vital and bright; full of life and energy. The photographs have turned out absolutely brilliantly!'

There were four different 'Ohs!' of surprise and disbelief.

'In fact, I've already rung the picture editor of the Sunday supplement and said that I want to do a special feature on her. He's agreed – he trusts my judgement – so next week's paper is going to be an Emily special!'

Total silence.

'I've got the proofs. Would you like to see them?'

'Well, er . . .' Mum said.

'Will there be any money in it?' Christopher asked.

'A fair amount,' the photographer replied. 'I think you'll be pleased; it's certainly enough for a lovely family holiday in the sun, and there should definitely be a modelling contract in the offing.' She hesitated. 'Is Katie around? It's all down to her, isn't it? I'm sure she'd like to see the proofs.'

There was another silence. I couldn't see them but I just knew they were all looking at each other in a meaningful, raised-eyebrow way.

After a long moment Mum called, 'Katie! Are you up there, love?'

'What *now*?' I called back in a weary sort of voice.

'If you could just come down please, Katie,' Helen called up (I say *called* but it was more like *cooed*).

'All right,' I said grudgingly, and then I straightened my tracksuit, patted my hair and, smiling a forgiving and loving smile, walked downstairs ready to receive everyone's apologies and grateful thanks. And also to help them plan a holiday in Disneyland . . .